Put Beginning Readers on the Right Track with
ALL ABOARD READING™

The All Aboard Reading series is especially designed for beginning readers. Written by noted authors and illustrated in full color, these are books that children really want to read—books to excite their imagination, expand their interests, make them laugh, and support their feelings. With fiction and nonfiction stories that are high interest and curriculum-related, All Aboard Reading books offer something for every young reader. And with four different reading levels, the All Aboard Reading series lets you choose which books are most appropriate for your children and their growing abilities.

Picture Readers
Picture Readers have super-simple texts, with many nouns appearing as rebus pictures. At the end of each book are 24 flash cards—on one side is a rebus picture; on the other side is the written-out word.

Station Stop 1
Station Stop 1 books are best for children who have just begun to read. Simple words and big type make these early reading experiences more comfortable. Picture clues help children to figure out the words on the page. Lots of repetition throughout the text helps children to predict the next word or phrase—an essential step in developing word recognition.

Station Stop 2
Station Stop 2 books are written specifically for children who are reading with help. Short sentences make it easier for early readers to understand what they are reading. Simple plots and simple dialogue help children with reading comprehension.

Station Stop 3
Station Stop 3 books are perfect for children who are reading alone. With longer text and harder words, these books appeal to children who have mastered basic reading skills. More complex stories captivate children who are ready for more challenging books.

In addition to All Aboard Reading books, look for All Aboard Math Readers™ (fiction stories that teach math concepts children are learning in school) and All Aboard Science Readers™ (nonfiction books that explore the most fascinating science topics in age-appropriate language).

All Aboard for happy reading!

Library of Congress Cataloging-in-Publication Data

Glassman, Jackie.
    The berry best friends' picnic / by Jackie Glassman ; illustrated by Ken Edwards and Gita Lloyd.
       p. cm. — (All aboard reading)
    "Strawberry Shortcake."
    Summary: When Strawberry and her friends prepare treats for a picnic they have to share ingredients with one another. [1. Sharing—Fiction. 2. Picnicking—Fiction.]
    I. Edwards, Ken, ill. II. Lloyd, Gita, ill. III. Title. IV. Series.
PZ7.G481433 Be 2003
[E]—dc21

                                        2002151241

ISBN 0-448-43134-3   B C D E F G H I J

The Berry Best Friends' Picnic

By Jackie Glassman
Cover illustrated by Lisa Workman
Illustrated by Ken Edwards and Gita Lloyd

Grosset & Dunlap • New York

Good morning,
Strawberry Shortcake.
Today is a berry sunny day!

Huckleberry Pie,
Orange Blossom,
Angel Cake,
and Ginger Snap
come over to play.

Woof! Woof!

Pupcake wants to have a picnic.

That is a <u>berry</u> good idea!

Everyone will make
a treat to share.

Everyone goes home
to get ready.

Strawberry Shortcake wants
to make a strawberry shortcake.
She needs strawberries,
cream,
and flour.

Uh-oh!
Strawberry Shortcake
has no flour!

But Angel Cake does.

Thank you, Angel Cake!

Angel Cake wants
to make frosting.
She needs milk,
sugar, and butter.

Uh-oh!

Angel Cake has no butter!

But Ginger Snap does.

Thank you, Ginger Snap!

Ginger Snap wants
to make jam cookies.
She needs butter,
sugar, and jam.

Uh-oh!

Ginger Snap has no jam!

But Huckleberry Pie does.

Thank you, Huckleberry Pie!

Huckleberry Pie wants
to make fruit punch.
He needs berries,
water, and oranges.

Uh-oh!
Huckleberry Pie
has no oranges!

But Orange Blossom
does. Thank you,
Orange Blossom!

Orange Blossom wants
to make fruit salad.
She needs oranges,
pears, and strawberries.
Uh-oh! Orange Blossom
has no strawberries.

But Strawberry Shortcake does.

Thank you,

Strawberry Shortcake!

It was <u>berry</u> good
that everyone shared.
They had the <u>berry</u> best
picnic ever!